Runaway Hamster

Runaway Hamster

Lucy Daniels

With special thanks to Janet Bingham

For Alicia. With thanks to Janice and Finn and

to Pauline and Bramble.

ORCHARD BOOKS

First published in Great Britain in 2019 by The Watts Publishing Group

1 3 5 7 9 10 8 6 4 2

Text copyright © Working Partners Ltd, 2019
Illustrations copyright © Working Partners Ltd, 2019

The moral rights of the author and illustrator have been asserted.

A CIP catalogue record for this book
is available from the British Library.

ISBN 978 1 40835 408 7

Printed and bound in Great Britain by CPI Group (UK) Ltd, Croydon, CR0 4YY

The paper and board used in this book are made from wood from responsible sources.

Orchard Books
An imprint of
Hachette Children's Group
Part of The Watts Publishing Group Limited
Carmelite House
50 Victoria Embankment
London EC4Y 0DZ

An Hachette UK Company
www.hachette.co.uk
www.hachettechildrens.co.uk

CONTENTS

CHAPTER ONE

"Here's your water, Sunny." Amelia
Haywood clipped a bottle to the front
of the pen. The fluffy grey rabbit stopped
chomping his dry food and took a drink.
Amelia tickled his nose through the wire.
"It's nice to see you happy again, now
that infection has cleared up."

Sam Baxter, Amelia's best friend, put
a dish of dog food into another pen and
patted the rough-haired terrier inside.
The little dog wagged her bandaged tail
cautiously. "Ruby's much better, too,"
said Sam. "I think she'll be going home
today."

It was Saturday morning. Amelia and
Sam were at Animal Ark, the veterinary
surgery in the village of Welford, helping
in the 'hotel'. It was the special room for
animals who needed to stay overnight.

Animal Ark was Amelia's favourite
place in the world. She and Sam had
worked hard to show the vets, Mr and
Mrs Hope, that they were responsible

enough to help out there. They came
in most days before school, and at the
weekend too. Amelia still tingled with
excitement every time she helped out at
Animal Ark.

"All done," Sam said. "Let's go and get Mac. He's been very quiet. I hope he isn't getting into any trouble!"

Mac was Sam's Westie puppy. When Amelia and Sam went into the reception room, they found him resting his front paws on Julia Kaminski's wheelchair. The receptionist laughed as she tickled his furry white chin. Mac's tongue lolled out and his stumpy tail flicked back and forth. Julia smiled at Sam and Amelia. "I just can't resist this puppy!"

"He can't

resist you either!" said Sam, grinning.

A man with a stubbly beard pushed the surgery door open with his shoulder. It was Mr Silva, whose family owned Welford's Indian restaurant. He was carrying a hamster travel case. After him came his daughters Lena and Sofia, who were two years below Amelia and Sam at school. They were identical twins but it wasn't hard to tell them apart – Lena's dark, wavy hair was in a ponytail and she wore a dress, while Sofia had shorter hair and was wearing jeans.

Julia smiled and said, "Good afternoon, Jay. Hello, girls. Who have you brought to see us today?"

"It's our hamster, Nibbles," said Lena. "He's poorly."

"He's not poorly," said her sister. "It's just that he's not hungry."

Mr Hope looked out of the examination room. "Is that Nibbles? You can bring him right in."

Amelia stepped forward quickly and held the door open for Mr Silva. Then she and Sam stood close to the

examination table, ready to help if Mr
Hope needed anything.

"I gather Nibbles isn't eating," said Mr
Hope. "How long has he been off his
food?"

"About a week," said Sofia.

"No," said Lena, shaking her head.
"It's been longer than that."

"He's lost quite a bit of weight," said
Mr Silva.

"How does he seem otherwise?" asked
Mr Hope.

"He's a bit quiet," said Lena.

"Only when you're too rough with
him," said Sofia.

"I'm not rough with him!" said Lena.

"Girls!" said their dad. "Let's not argue, please."

His daughters nodded sulkily.

Mr Hope opened the carrier and lifted out a sleepy golden hamster. Nibbles blinked blearily and nudged his nose down between Mr Hope's fingers, as if he were trying to burrow back into a cosy nest.

"Let's have a look at Nibbles's teeth and pouches," said Mr Hope. He held the scruff of the hamster's neck between his thumb and forefinger, and gently turned him upside down in the palm of his other hand.

Nibbles's mouth opened to show four

long, pointed teeth and a strong tongue.

Amelia could see lots of pink skin

inside his cheeks, which she knew could

balloon into pouches to carry food.

Mr Hope nodded. "Nice teeth, not

overgrown."

"They're yellow," said Sofia. "My

dentist said yellow teeth were bad."

"That's true for people," said Mr

Hope, "but hamster teeth are meant to be yellow."

Lena nudged her sister. "See? I told you so!"

"His mouth and nose look good," Mr Hope went on. "But he is rather thin. Is he drinking plenty of water?"

"Yes," said Lena.

"No," said Sofia.

Mr Hope looked at the twins questioningly.

"Well, sometimes," admitted Sofia.

"He doesn't look dehydrated," said Mr Hope. "So that's good." He checked Nibbles all over, looking carefully at his bottom. "His fur is in good condition.

There's no sign of wet tail."

"What's that?" asked Amelia.

"A stress-related condition," said Mr Hope. "It's rather unpleasant."

Mr Hope put Nibbles back in the carrier. The little animal pushed his pink nose through the holes and Amelia stroked the long, fine whiskers vibrating around his cheeks.

"What do you feed him?" asked Mr Hope.

"Hamster food," said Sofia.

"Well, duh!" said Lena, rolling her eyes.

"What type of hamster food?" asked Mr Hope patiently.

"It says 'Hamster Feast' on the packet," explained Sofia. "We buy it at the pet shop. It's got seeds in it, and bits of corn and little round biscuits …"

"Dry food specially made for hamsters is very good," said Mr Hope. "But he might need something else to encourage him to eat."

"What do you suggest?" asked Mr Silva.

"A bit of fruit or vegetables. Grapes and apples are good, and I've never met a hamster who didn't love a slice of carrot."

Mr Silva chuckled. "Well, our house is full of food at the moment. My wife and I are running a stall at tomorrow's food fair at Welford Common. We've been cooking curries for days."

Mr Hope laughed. "Well, don't give Nibbles any curry. But it sounds as if you'll find plenty to tempt him. You could try a tiny bit of hard cheese or some boiled egg, too."

"I hope you'll all come to the fair tomorrow," said Mr Silva. "There will be games and prizes, as well as lots of delicious food! I recommend the tandoori chicken. It's our speciality!"

Amelia's stomach rumbled. "We'll be there!"

Mr Silva turned back to Mr Hope.

"We'll let you know how Nibbles gets on with his new diet."

"I'll carry him," said Lena, reaching for the hamster carrier.

"No, I will," said Sofia, trying to grab the handle.

Mr Silva picked up the carrier himself and shooed his daughters out of the surgery.

Amelia caught Sam's eye and he shrugged. She knew he was thinking the same as her: *The twins just can't stop arguing!*

CHAPTER TWO

Amelia and Sam followed the Silva
family into the reception room, where
Mrs Hope was talking to Julia.

"Who's our next appointment?" asked
Mrs Hope.

The receptionist looked at her screen.
"Annie Stein and Kate Grey. They're

bringing in their four micro pigs for a
check-up."

Amelia's cheeks grew warm with
excitement. "Oh, wow! I've never seen a
micro pig!"

"Me neither," said Sam. "How big are
they?"

"Very young ones can fit in a teacup,"
Mrs Hope replied. "They usually grow to
be a bit bigger than Mac."

A woman with curly hair bundled
through the door. She was leading
two small pigs wearing pretty yellow
harnesses.

Amelia gasped. "They're so cute!"

The pigs were pink with black spots.

They had upturned snouts, floppy ears and corkscrew tails. They looked as if they were tiptoeing on their dainty trotters. Mac watched them with an inquisitive whine.

A tall woman with short hair followed them in, holding two thick leather leads. From outside the door came loud gasps, snorts and grunts.

Amelia nudged Sam. "It sounds like she's brought a couple of hippos!"

In waddled two more pigs. Like the first two, they were pink with black spots, floppy ears and curly tails. But that was where the similarity ended. *Never mind a teacup*, thought Amelia. *These pigs would barely fit in a bathtub!*

"Whoa," whispered Sam. "Those aren't micro pigs …"

"They're *massive* pigs!" said Amelia.

The big pigs started exploring the reception area, pulling their owner after

them. One of them waddled up to Mac, who backed away and hid behind Sam's ankles. The other snuffled across the floor, knocking over a rack of leaflets with its hefty rump.

The pig's owner gave an embarrassed

laugh. "Sorry! Stop that, Daisy!"

Mac whimpered and Sam knelt down to stroke him. "It's all right, Mac. The pigs are just curious."

Meanwhile, the two little pigs were prancing around the other lady, tying her legs together with their leads as they oinked loudly.

"Help!" she cried.

One pig shot forward. The lady tottered, then tumbled over, dropping the leads. The two little pigs raced for the door. Amelia sprinted to catch one, while Sam lunged for the other. Amelia clutched the struggling pig tightly to her chest. He scrabbled around and nuzzled

her face with his
flat, wet nose.
Amelia laughed
and scratched the

bristly skin behind his ears.

"Oh gosh!" sighed the woman, getting
back to her feet. "We're so sorry! I'm
Annie, by the way."

"And I'm Kate," the other woman
said. She gave Amelia and Sam a
flustered smile. "Thank you for catching
Tammy and Tim. They can be so
naughty."

Mr and Mrs Hope helped the
ladies coax the two big pigs into the
examination room, while Amelia and

Sam followed, carrying the two little ones.
They placed them on the examination
table. The two large pigs stood on the floor
– they were almost as big as the table!

"Let's give the pigs a check-up," said Mr
Hope. "I'll start with the big ones – Pip
and Daisy, isn't it? I might as well, because
I can't move …"

Pip's big trotter was pinning Mr Hope's
foot to the floor. Amelia
gave the pig's bristly leg a

friendly tickle. He swung his head towards her and lifted his foot.

"Phew!" said Mr Hope, kneeling down.

Mrs Hope started to examine the smaller pigs. "Amelia, could you pass the otoscope?" she asked. Amelia felt a burst of pride as she fetched the little hammer-shaped instrument from the shelf. Mrs Hope peered through it into Tim's ears.

Sam was holding Tammy on the table, ready for her turn. "I didn't know that micro pigs grew so big."

Kate smiled. "Believe it or not, they were all tiny when they were piglets. But there was a mix-up. It turned out they came from two different litters. Daisy and Pip aren't micro pigs at all. It was a shock when they didn't stop growing!"

Amelia patted Daisy's bristly shoulder. "Do they live in your house?"

"Oh no," said Annie. "Even though they're pets, they like being outside in the garden, so they can snuffle in the earth."

"We had plenty of room when they were all tiny," added Kate. "But not now."

After a while, the vets finished the check-up. "Pip and Daisy are in excellent health," declared Mr Hope.

Mrs Hope nodded. "Tammy and Tim are too."

"That's brilliant," said Annie. She scratched Daisy's neck. "Now to get you piggies back home …" She and Kate gathered up the pigs' leads and struggled out of the examination room.

Amelia and Sam followed them out into the reception area. One of the big pigs was snuffling at something under Julia's desk. Kate tugged on the lead. "Chop chop, Daisy."

Daisy turned and trotted the other

way at speed, almost yanking her
owner off her feet.

Amelia and Sam glanced at each
other, then darted forward. "We can
help you get home!" offered Amelia. "If
that's OK?"

Mr Hope nodded. "Of course!"

Kate flashed them a grateful smile.
"That would be great." She gave Amelia
and Sam the micro pigs' leads, while
she and Annie each took one of the big
pigs.

Sam collected Mac on the way out,
and in a few moments they were all
walking up the road. Amelia glanced
down at Tammy and Tim, trotting

briskly beside them. She nudged Sam.
"These pigs walk to heel just like Mac!"

"Pigs are actually quite easy to train,"
said Annie. "They're really intelligent
animals."

But when they walked across the
village green, the big pigs sped up. Annie

and Kate broke into a run as they tried to keep up with them.

Amelia felt Tim tug on his lead, then suddenly it went slack. She looked down and gasped. Tim had pulled free of his collar! He was sprinting to the flowerbed, his curly tail bouncing.

"Quick, Sam!" Amelia cried. "We've got to catch him!"

CHAPTER THREE

They sprinted after Tim, with Mac and
Tammy trotting beside them. Tim broke
into a gallop and took a flying leap …

Splat! The micro pig landed in the
flowerbed. Grunting happily, he rolled
over in the mud, crushing several plants.
Then he started munching on the leaves

and petals. Amelia grabbed Tim around his firm little tummy and tried to pull him away. He gave a squeal of protest and wriggled free. Then Tammy jumped into the flowerbed, too, while Mac ran around, barking with excitement.

"Oh no!" groaned Sam. "The other two are coming!"

Daisy and Pip, dragging their owners with them, thundered into the flowerbed. They bulldozed through the soil, chomping on plant stems and digging up roots. Clods of earth flew everywhere. Amelia rubbed splatters of mud off her face and stared in dismay. The flowerbed looked like a disaster zone!

Annie and Kate caught up with them. Kate's cheeks were flushed red. "Stop! Stop!" she shouted.

"Naughty pigs!" cried Annie, her hair dishevelled.

The pigs' owners fumbled in their pockets for treats and held them out, calling, "Here, piggies!"

Even with the treats, it was a long time before they managed to coax the pigs out of the flowerbed. Annie stared at the ruined plants in dismay. "Look at this mess! We'd better call the council and apologise. But first let's get the pigs home before they do any more damage!"

The two women lived in a bungalow at the end of a winding lane. They led everyone through a gate into the back garden.

"Whoa!" Sam whispered to Amelia. "No flowers here!"

The garden was a patch of mud covered in trotter-prints and surrounded by a thick hedge. A fence divided it into two sections — a big section with a large pigsty, and a small section with a little pigsty. Kate shooed Pip and Daisy into the big section and Tammy and Tim into the little one.

"Don't they all live together?" asked Amelia in surprise.

Annie shook her head. "Pigs prefer to be with other pigs the same size as them," she explained.

"They'd be even happier with more space," said Kate. "But they're already taking up the whole garden and we can't afford to move."

The pigs were still covered in mud, so

Amelia wasn't surprised when Annie announced, "Bath time!"

Kate brought out a pink plastic paddling pool. Sam and Amelia held on to Tim and Tammy, who wriggled with excitement while Annie filled the pool from a hosepipe. When it was full, Amelia and Sam let go of the little pigs and they dived in. Mac leaped in, too. The three of them splashed about in the shallow water, rolling around and climbing over each other.

"Want to give the pigs a scrub?" asked Kate, holding up a pair of brushes.

"Yes!" Amelia and Sam both cried. They pulled off their shoes and socks

and waded in. Sam grabbed Tammy,
and Amelia caught Tim. The little pig
stood quietly, grunting contentedly as
she rubbed him with the bristly brush.
Amelia glanced up at Sam and giggled.
He was washing Tammy but also giving
Mac a few quick scrubs.

The big pigs watched through the fence, squealing impatiently.

"Your turn now, Pip and Daisy!" called Annie. "Time for a shower." She sprayed the hosepipe at them and the two big pigs jostled against each other, water running down their sides as they grunted with delight.

"I thought pigs liked being dirty," said Sam.

"A lot of people think that," said Kate. "Pigs do love a good wallow – mud cools them down and helps them get rid of fleas. But they like a wash afterwards."

When the pigs were clean, Annie and Kate lifted Tammy and Tim out of their bath and let Amelia and Sam rub them dry with towels. Amelia shook the water off her legs. When everyone was reasonably dry, the four pigs tucked into more piggy treats.

Amelia peered at one of the biscuits the pigs were eating. "Is that a flapjack?"

"Sort of," said Kate. "We make them ourselves from oats, with raisins and pumpkin seeds."

Amelia smiled as Tammy gobbled a treat from the palm of her hand. She suddenly remembered Lena and Sofia's hamster.

An idea popped into her head.

"Sam!" she said. "I know how we can help Nibbles …"

Early the next morning, Amelia came downstairs to the smell of cooking. Her kitten, Star, was in the kitchen, staring hopefully at Amelia's gran as she spooned something from a steaming saucepan into pastry shells.

"Smells delicious!" said Amelia.

"I'm making mini chicken pies for the baking contest at the food fair," said her gran.

"Come on," said Amelia, stroking Star. "Let's get you some of your own food."

She opened a sachet of food and put it in a bowl. While Star ate, Amelia's gran opened the oven and took out a tray of golden-crusted pies.

"The first batch look good!" said Mum, coming into the kitchen.

Gran turned out one of the pies on to a plate and cut it into quarters, waving the steam away to cool it down. "Have a taste. What do you think?"

Amelia nibbled the cooling pastry. "It's delicious. You've put something different in, haven't you?"

Gran nodded. "My secret ingredient – a herb called marjoram." She tasted a piece. "Hmm … It still needs something else. Let me think …" She began to bustle about, peering into the cupboards.

Her mum smiled. "Gran's in the zone now."

Amelia grinned at her mum. "I'm going to head over to Sam's if that's OK."

"That's fine," said Mum. "See you at the food fair later!"

CHAPTER FOUR

Sam and his parents lived at the Old
Mill Bed and Breakfast. The kitchen
there was big, as it was where Sam's dad
cooked for the guests. Sam had propped
his mum's tablet up on the worktop so
he and Amelia could watch a video
explaining how to make hamster treats.

"*You will need flour, water, banana and peanut butter*," said the woman presenting the video. "*Oh, and hamsters love mixed seeds too ...*"

Sam rifled in the cupboards and pulled out the ingredients. "Let's get started!"

They mashed the banana in a bowl and stirred in the water, peanut butter and poppy seeds. Next they added the flour slowly, mixing everything up with their hands to make a sticky dough. Amelia pinched a piece off, rolled it between her palms and squished it into a biscuit shape. She held it up triumphantly. "Ta da!"

Mac gave an excited whine. "Sorry, Mac," said Sam. "These are hamster treats, not puppy treats!"

They made the rest of the biscuits, then laid them on a baking tray. Amelia set the timer as Sam's dad popped them into the oven.

While the hamster treats baked, they went out into the garden and threw

a ball for Mac. He scampered around fetching it, until they heard the timer go off from inside the kitchen.

"The treats are done!" said Amelia.

They hurried back inside and asked Sam's dad to take the tray out of the oven. The biscuits actually smelled quite nice, even though they were meant for hamsters.

There was a knock at the back door, and a bald head poked through. Mr Ferguson was a regular guest at the Old Mill. "I'm looking for my motorcycle gloves. Mac hasn't run off with them again, has he?"

"I don't think so," said Sam.

"Maybe I left them in my room," said Mr Ferguson. He spied the treats cooling on the tray. "Don't mind if I do!" he said. Before they could stop him, he reached over and popped one in his mouth. "Hmmm," he said, crunching on the hamster treat.

"How are they?" asked Amelia, fighting back her giggles.

Mr Ferguson frowned. "I'm not sure they'll win any prizes, to be honest. But they're quite tasty."

Mr Ferguson helped himself to a

second treat and left, calling over his shoulder, "See you at the fair later!"

The restaurant owned by the Silva family was at the other end of Welford. Sam took Mac on his lead, while Amelia carried the hamster treats. They rattled around in a plastic tub, and Mac kept glancing at them hopefully.

Sam laughed. "Now I know how to make Mac walk perfectly to heel. I just need to carry hamster treats with me wherever I go!"

Amelia grinned back at him. "It's lucky we met those pigs," she said.

"I would never have thought of making hamster treats otherwise!"

As they passed the farmhouse where the Parish family lived, they saw their friend Caleb. He was perched on the fence, watching his two pet llamas, Llarry and Lliam, grazing.

"Are you coming to the food fair?" asked Sam.

Their friend nodded. "Mum's made marmalades," he said. "And Dad's been sewing funky aprons!"

Caleb's dad was a fashion designer. Amelia wondered if she could buy one of his aprons for her gran's birthday.

"The llamas look like they're enjoying

their new home," Amelia said, watching
the llamas munch grass.

"Yeah, they love it," Caleb replied.
"They've got lots of space. We could have
a whole herd of llamas in this field!"

Looking at the wide open space,
Amelia remembered Daisy and Pip.
The big pigs were crammed into their
little garden. *I wonder* … she thought.

"Caleb," Amelia said, "do you like pigs?"

"I love pigs!" he said. "Why?"

Amelia explained Annie and Kate's problem, then pointed at the paddock. "All the pigs need is a big patch of mud and a pen."

Caleb hopped down from the fence. "I'll go and see what Dad thinks!" He ran off towards his house.

WOOF!

Amelia looked round to see why Mac was barking. Her heart sank. Tiffany Banks and her puppy Sparkle were walking up the road. Tiffany went to the same school as Sam and Amelia.

She wasn't very friendly, but Sparkle
loved to play. He wagged his tail and
jumped around, making the blue bow
on top of his fluffy white head bounce.

Sam sighed. "Looks like Sparkle wants
to say hello …"

The two puppies greeted each other
with snuffles and barks.

Tiffany sniffed. "Your grubby puppy

better not make Sparkle's fur dirty."

Why does she always have to be so horrible? thought Amelia. Then she reminded herself that just because Tiffany wasn't nice didn't mean Amelia couldn't be friendly. She noticed Tiffany was holding a plastic tub like hers. "What's in your tub?"

"Macaroons for the food fair," said Tiffany. "I made them this morning."

She opened the tub. Inside were perfect, dainty round biscuits in pastel colours – pink, green and yellow.

"They look amazing," said Sam.

"I know," said Tiffany smugly. "So what have you made?"

Amelia opened the tub to reveal the lumpy hamster treats.

Tiffany sniggered. "Yuck! Those look gross! Who would want to eat them?"

Amelia pushed the lid back on.

"They're not for people," said Sam. "We made them for a poorly hamster."

"Anyway, it's not how they look that counts," snapped Amelia. "It's how they taste."

Tiffany smirked. "Well you'd better hope a hamster's judging the baking contest," she said. Then she tossed her ponytail and stomped off, Sparkle trailing after her.

CHAPTER FIVE

The front door to the restaurant was locked when they arrived, but Amelia could hear noises coming from the rear. They found a back door open, and the air was thick with spicy cooking smells. Mr Silva was carrying a box from the kitchen to a van.

"Hello!" he said. "I'm afraid the restaurant isn't open today."

"Actually, we came to see the twins," said Amelia.

"Inside!" said their dad, nodding to the door. "Arguing, no doubt."

Sam tied Mac to a fencepost outside and told him to 'stay'. Inside the back door, Mrs Silva was wearing her chef's whites and looking after several pots on the stove. She opened the top of a huge clay oven and used a pair of tongs to take out naan breads, then rushed over to where meat was grilling on skewers over charcoal.

"What's next?" asked Mr Silva as he

came back into the kitchen.

"Check that saucepan!" said Mrs
Silva. "It mustn't stick!"

"Which one?" said Mr Silva. There
were three pans of curry on the stove, all
bubbling away.

"The masala!" said his wife.

Mr Silva took a spoon and stirred.

"Don't forget the tub of coriander in the fridge," said his wife as she flipped the skewers then squirted the grill with water. Smoke billowed into the air, enveloping everyone.

Mrs Silva wiped her forehead. "How long until the food fair starts?"

Sam checked his watch. "About an hour."

"Oh gosh!" said Mrs Silva. "We're cutting it fine!" She began to lay the naan breads in a cardboard box.

Mr Silva grinned at Amelia and Sam. "I'd get out of here, if I were you. Otherwise she'll give you a job as well."

Sam and Amelia went up the stairs

leading to the family's flat above the restaurant. When they were halfway up, Amelia heard music and the sound of Lena and Sofia's voices from above.

"You said I could watch my programme!"

"When this song's finished!"

"You've been listening to it on repeat all day!"

"Don't exaggerate!"

"Just put your headphones in."

Amelia knocked and pushed the door open. Lena and Sofia were scowling at each other. But when they saw Sam and Amelia, their faces broke into smiles. "Hi!" they said at the same time.

Amelia popped the lid off the tub, and held it out proudly. The twins stared into it. Sofia wrinkled her nose. "Are they biscuits?"

"Hamster treats," Amelia said. "For Nibbles!"

The twins leapt up in delight. "Whoa! Thank you, that's amazing!" cried Lena.

"We thought they might get him to eat," explained Sam.

Amelia felt something nudge her foot. She looked down and saw a clear plastic ball with a little golden hamster running inside, pushing the ball along. It bumped into a chair, and the hamster sat up and rubbed his paws. Then he turned around,

and the ball rolled
towards the door.

Amelia grinned.
"It looks like
Nibbles is feeling
better! Shall we see
what he thinks of the treats?"

"Oh, that's not Nibbles," said Sofia. "It's
Nacho."

Amelia caught Sam's confused
expression. "Nacho?" she asked. "Have
you got two hamsters?"

"Yes," said Lena. "Nibbles is in his own
ball – he went behind the sofa …"

Amelia leaned over the sofa and saw
the hamster ball, but it was empty. Its

small door was hanging open. "Er, guys
– he's not in there," she said.

Both twins scrambled over to look.

"You must not have closed it properly,"
Lena accused her sister.

"I put Nacho in his!" said Sofia. "You
did Nibbles."

"No I didn't!"

"It doesn't matter," interrupted Sam.

The twins looked at each other. "We have to find him!" said Lena.

"OK, let's not panic," said Amelia, glancing around the floor. Hopefully Nibbles hadn't gone far.

They searched under the armchairs and the sofa, but there was no sign of the hamster. Then Lena and Sofia checked the kitchen and the bathroom. When they came back into the living room, Lena's bottom lip began to quiver.

"Nothing," said Sofia, her eyes filled with tears.

"Don't worry," Amelia said quickly. "I'm sure we'll find him."

"Where's his cage?" asked Sam.

"In our bedroom," said Sofia. "It's on the next floor up, but Nibbles is good at climbing."

She led Amelia and Sam towards the stairs, but Sofia said crossly, "Lena, you forgot Nacho. Don't you care if we lose him too?" She picked up the other hamster in his ball, pushed past Lena and stomped up the stairs.

Lena glowered. "Well, at least I shut Nacho's ball properly."

"No, that was *me*!"

"It doesn't matter whose fault it is," Amelia interrupted. "Poor Nibbles is lost and we need to find him."

The twins' bedroom was cramped

and untidy. Bunk beds, one piled with a messy duvet and tangled pyjamas, the other neatly made, stood against one wall. One half of the floor was littered with toys and clothes, the other was spotless, with books arranged on a shelf and toys in a line. There was a hamster cage on the floor by the window. It wasn't very big and was crammed with climbing ramps, chewed cardboard tubes, a wheel, a litter tray and a food bowl. The bottom was lined with wood chippings and sawdust.

Lena checked inside and shook her head. "He's not in here."

Sofia opened the hamster ball and let

Nacho climb into the cage.

"Do Nibbles and Nacho both live in this cage?" Amelia asked.

Lena nodded. "They're brothers," she

explained. "So they like living together."

Amelia wasn't sure about that. She thought of Daisy and Pip again, all cramped in their pen.

"We'd better check in Mum and Dad's room," said Lena.

After the sisters had left, Amelia turned to Sam and whispered, "I'm pretty sure Mrs Hope told me that hamsters need their own space."

Sam raised his eyebrows, glancing at the bunk beds. "I think Lena and Sofia do as well!"

CHAPTER SIX

Inside the cage, Nacho headed for the food bowl. He picked up a sunflower seed and began to nibble it, turning it in his front paws until the stripy shell fell away. He ate the kernel inside and then nibbled on some oats. After he'd eaten half the bowlful, he began filling his cheek pouches with the rest. His face stretched wider and wider until the bowl was empty.

Amelia frowned. *Nacho's taking all the food and there's none left for Nibbles — maybe that's why he's so skinny.*

Just then Lena and her sister returned. "He's not in there either!"

"Let's look in the living room again," Amelia suggested. "We might have missed a clue."

Back downstairs, they spread out, searching the floor on their hands and knees. There was no sign of Nibbles.

"He can't just have disappeared!" said Sam.

The door opened and Mr Silva came in. "Right, girls, we're about to set off for the fair. Do you want to …" He must have noticed their distressed faces. "What's the matter?"

"Lena lost Nibbles," said Sofia.

"No, Sofia lost Nibbles!" said Lena.

Amelia cut in before another argument could start. "We think he must be in the apartment somewhere," she said, "because the door to the restaurant was closed."

Mr Silva put a hand to his mouth. "Oh no!" he said. "It's closed normally, but I propped it open earlier, because I was carrying things up and down the stairs."

"Nibbles might have escaped," wailed Lena.

They all crowded into the restaurant downstairs.

"You go ahead," Mr Silva told his wife. "I'll stay here and help look for Nibbles."

As Mrs Silva drove off in the van, the rest of them checked the restaurant carefully, under all the tables and behind the bar, but there was no sign of Nibbles.

That left only the kitchen. The sink was piled high with dirty pots and pans.

"Look!" cried Sofia. "I found something."

There was a little pile of black pellets on the floor and a few bits of what looked like wet cardboard.

"Isn't that where the box of naan breads was?" said Sam.

Mr Silva's eyes went wide. "You're right! It looks like Nibbles might have eaten his way inside!" He pulled out his mobile phone and called his wife. He shook his head. "She's not answering!"

Amelia frowned. "If Nibbles gets out on Welford Common, we'll never get him back!"

The twins gasped in horror.

Amelia sprinted for the door. "Come on!" she called to the others. "We've got to get to the food fair before Nibbles escapes."

They ran all the way to Welford Common. Mac raced ahead, tail wagging. Soon Amelia could smell a mixture of delicious smells – sweet and spicy, fruity and savoury.

On the common there were several

stalls set up around a huge main tent. It was open on one side and filled with rows of trestle tables. There was a raised platform at one end. On it stood the mayor, testing out the sound system.

"Check one two," he said into a microphone.

When they reached the stalls, Amelia could see every kind of food imaginable, from chutneys and chocolates to sausages and stews. She sniffed the air, trying to catch the scent of curry.

Mac tried to pull Sam over to a stall where a man was grilling hot dogs, but Sam tugged him back. "There's no time for sausages, Mac. We're looking for Mrs

Silva's stall." Standing on his tiptoes, he looked over the heads of the visitors and pointed inside the tent. "There it is, Amelia!"

They hurried in past Gran, who was carrying one of her chicken pies to the baking contest. "Hi, kids," she said. "Where are you—"

"Sorry, Gran!" Amelia called as

they ran past. "We've got a hamster emergency!"

She passed Farmer Stevens's vegetable stall and almost ran straight into Caleb's dad. Mr Parish sidestepped her, his arms draped with brightly coloured aprons.

I wonder if Caleb managed to ask him about the pigs … Amelia thought as she raced past. But there wasn't time to stop.

Mr and Mrs Hope were at the next table, laying out plates of pawprint-shaped biscuits. They waved at Amelia and Sam as they sprinted past.

"Can't stop," panted Sam. "We're hamster-hunting!"

Mrs Silva was still setting up, with curry pots simmering on gas burners and bhajis warming in a small portable heater.

"You're in a rush!" said Mrs Silva. "Did you want some curry?"

"Where's the box of naan bread?" asked Amelia.

"Under here," Mrs Silva said, pointing to her feet.

Amelia leaned over the table and saw the box. The lid was hanging open. *Oh no*, she thought, horrified. *Nibbles must have crawled out!*

Lena and Sofia came running up. Sofia gasped. "There he is!"

By one of the table legs, Nibbles was chewing on a small bit of naan bread. His tiny eyes gleamed and his whiskers quivered. Amelia scrambled to reach him, but Nibbles sprinted away through the busy tent.

"Catch him!" cried Sam.

They all dashed after the hamster.

"What's going on?" called Mrs
Silva, but there was no time to stop
and explain. Nibbles appeared and
disappeared around people's legs and
under tables, as Amelia, Sam and the
twins ran to keep up. The hamster
darted under a pushchair. The little boy
inside giggled and pointed as it ran
out the other side. Then
Nibbles reached the
edge of the tent, and
darted underneath
the side.

"He's gone
outside!" said
Amelia.

They sprinted out of the tent, on to the grass.

"Look!" yelled Sam. "The juice stall!"

A man with a ginger beard was almost hidden behind piles of fruit and vegetables ready for blitzing in the juicers that stood on a table. A pyramid of apples was piled beside the stall, and scrambling up them like a ladder, was Nibbles.

Still running, Amelia shouted, "Hey!"

The stallholder's mouth dropped open when he noticed Nibbles sitting like a furry golden apple on top of all the green and red ones. He reached to pick him up, but Nibbles was too quick for him. The little hamster leaped on to the table, vanishing among the piles of carrots and kale.

The man lunged to catch him again, but missed – and bumped into the table. The fruit wobbled and then …

THUMP! A large pineapple landed on the ground.

SPLAT! Several mangoes and some pears fell too.

WHUMPH! The pile of apples collapsed and fruit tumbled everywhere. Apples rolled under Amelia's feet and she stumbled, arms whirling. Behind her, Sam floundered as his legs went in different directions. Mac ran around them, barking and chasing after the fruit.

"OOF!" yelped Amelia. She and Sam landed on their bottoms, apples all around them.

The stallholder stared in dismay at the scattered fruit. "Was that a ... mouse?"

"We're really sorry about the mess," said Amelia, scrambling up and hauling Sam to his feet. "We'll explain later!"

They searched the area around the juice stall desperately – and saw Nibbles race into a crowd of people. Amelia felt a rush of cold fear as Nibbles weaved around the shoes and boots, then darted back towards the tent. "He'll be trodden on!" said Amelia.

A large Alsatian began to bark, straining on his lead as Nibbles ran past.

"Or eaten!" said Sam.

Amelia suddenly had an idea. She dashed into the tent and climbed up on the stage. Then she snatched the

microphone away from the mayor.
"Help!" she yelled into it, her voice
ringing out across the tent. "Catch that
hamster!"

CHAPTER SEVEN

Everyone stared at Amelia in surprise,
including the mayor, a portly man
wearing his gleaming chains of office.

"A hamster?" asked a woman
munching a chocolate-filled pancake.
"How did a hamster get in here?"

"It's a long story," Amelia said, into

the microphone. She saw Lena and
Sofia searching the ground, worried
looks on their faces. "But we need to get
him home safely. His owners really miss
him. Please help us catch Nibbles!"

There were murmurs of agreement
and the crowd began searching the

tent, treading carefully. Amelia saw Mr
and Mrs Hope joining in the search. If
anything bad did happen to Nibbles, at
least they'd be on hand to help.

"He's here!" called a teenage girl
holding an ice cream.

"He went under that table!" said a

man selling stinky cheeses.

"Now he's behind those crates," yelled someone else.

"Eeeek!"

Amelia whirled round. Mrs Cranbourne, an elderly lady who lived in the village, was flapping a tea towel at her cake stand. "Get off my cakes!" she screeched. "Shoo!"

Amelia and Sam dashed over. Mr Ferguson was tucking into a cookie.

"Not as good as your biscuits!" he said through a mouthful of crumbs.

Fruit cakes, Swiss rolls, carrot cakes and cupcakes were arranged on the table. One was decorated with white icing, which had a pattern that looked like tiny pawprints in freshly fallen snow. Amelia leaned closer. They *were* pawprints!

The trail of icing pawprints led to the edge of the table and down a stack of boxes filled with paper plates and napkins. Amelia and Sam followed the trail. And there, already racing out of the tent, was Nibbles.

Sam slapped his forehead. "Not again!"

Amelia groaned. "We're never going to catch him, are we?"

They dashed out of the tent just in time to see something pink fly through the air. A macaroon landed on the grass, but Nibbles ran past it.

"Don't you want a treat?" called Tiffany. "They're really good." She tossed another macaroon in the air – a green one. This time Nibbles stopped running and sniffed it.

Amelia held her breath. Whiskers twitching, Nibbles began to chew at the edge of the macaroon.

Quick as a flash, Amelia scooped the

hamster up and passed him to Lena.
For a moment she expected Sofia to
complain, but for once the twins didn't
argue. Nibbles was still munching the
macaroon.

"Wow, Tiffany," whispered Amelia.
"You did it."

"Of course I did," said Tiffany
triumphantly. "My macaroons are
irresistible."

"Thank you!" Sofia threw her arms around Tiffany and hugged her. "You saved our pet."

"You're a hero," said Lena. She passed Nibbles to her sister. "Here, you hold him now. He should know we're both here." Sofia smiled at her sister as they both stroked their pet.

"It's good to see him eating!" said Sam.

It's good to see the twins getting along too, thought Amelia.

"Do you want one too?" asked Tiffany, holding out the plate of macaroons to the girls and Sam.

"Are you sure?" asked Amelia. "Don't you need them for the baking contest?"

Tiffany shrugged. "It's OK. Pets are more important than baking contests. I'd hate it if I lost Sparkle."

They all took a macaroon.

"Mmm," said Lena. "Yummy."

"They're delicious," said Sam.

Amelia nodded, her mouth too full to say anything.

Tiffany blushed and looked embarrassed.

Mr Silva walked up, waving an empty plastic tub. "Sofia, pop Nibbles in here. I've made air-holes in the lid. I expect

he's exhausted after his adventure."
Sofia gently put Nibbles inside, and he
immediately curled up. "Go and enjoy
yourselves," said the twins' dad. "I'll look
after Nibbles."

The twins went off to play with
some kids from their class and Tiffany
wandered over to look at Mr Parish's
aprons.

"I'm starving!" said Sam. "Let's get
something to eat."

"What are you in the mood for?"
asked Amelia, her tummy rumbling.

Sam chuckled. "Anything except
apples! How about curry?" Mac barked
as if he agreed.

Amelia and Sam went over to Mrs
Silva's stand. They joined the queue
and studied the menu written on a
blackboard.

"Chicken korma, please," said Amelia.

"I'll have tandoori lamb," said Sam.

"I'm afraid you'll have to have it with
rice!" said Mrs Silva. "I've had to throw
away the naan breads, but at least
Nibbles is safe and sound."

She handed them their food and
shook her head when they tried to pay.
"It's on the house," she said, smiling.
"To say thank you for helping us find
Nibbles."

Amelia and Sam found an empty

patch of grass and ate their spicy food.
Afterwards they each had an ice cream,
then joined the crowd gathering in the
big tent for the prize ceremony. Amelia
and Sam went over to stand with Gran,
who gave them a nervous smile.

"Good luck," Amelia told her.

The mayor announced the winners
of the baking contest. Amelia held
her breath when it came to the
announcement for the pie section. The
mayor cleared his throat. "First prize
goes to …Colette! For her delectable
chicken pie!"

Amelia whooped and cheered. Gran's
hands flew to her face, but they couldn't

hide her smile. She
hurried up to collect
her prize and came
back with a shiny
red pie dish.

"Congratulations,
Gran," said Amelia,
hugging her.

Then the mayor
said, "And now we have a special prize
for a quick-witted young lady who
helped with today's pet rescue. Tiffany!
Please come and get your reward!"

Tiffany went to the front and Amelia
cheered loudly with everyone else as the
mayor handed her a box of chocolates.

For once, Tiffany was smiling.

"It was nice of Tiffany to help us catch Nibbles," whispered Sam.

Amelia nodded. Today she'd seen a different side of Tiffany. *Maybe she isn't so bad after all?*

CHAPTER EIGHT

After the fair had finished, Sam and
Amelia stayed behind for a while to help
the Silvas clear up. Nibbles was sleeping
safely in his box.

"He must be tired from all that running
around!" said Sam.

"And his tummy is full of yummy

macaroons!" said Lena, laughing.

Amelia and Sam walked home together with Mac, and as soon as they went through the door the smell of sweet pastry hit their noses. It made Amelia's stomach rumble.

They went into the kitchen to find Gran taking her new pie dish out of the oven.

"I can't believe you're baking again," said Amelia.

"A nice man from the juice stall gave me loads of apples," said Gran. "He said they were too bruised for him to use!"

"Er, that might have been our fault," muttered Sam.

Amelia and Sam tucked into the
steaming pie, with some thick cream
from the fridge. Star came and looked
up at Amelia with a sad, pleading *meow*.
The kitten seemed to have crumbs on
her whiskers.

"Gran, has Star been eating apple pie?"

"Mm-hmm," said Gran, looking a
little bit guilty. "Just one or two bits. She
looked hungry!"

Sam snorted with laughter. "That sounds just like Mac. You'd think he was starving!"

Amelia stroked Star's soft black-and-ginger fur and let her lap up the leftover cream. "Who's a little piggy?" she cooed. She turned back to Sam and grinned. "That reminds me. We've got some plans to make ..."

A few days later Amelia and Sam were at the Parishes' house with Caleb, helping to make a scratching post. Mr and Mrs Parish had fenced off part of one field and built a roomy pigsty inside it. The scratching post in the middle of the pen was the finishing touch.

Annie and Kate were chatting with Mrs Parish. Llarry and Lliam, the llamas, stood on the other side of the fence, peering over like nosy neighbours.

Daisy and Pip snuffled about excitedly in their new pen as Amelia banged the final nail into the post. "All done," she said, and stepped out of the way as Daisy gave her an impatient shove.

The scratching post was a wooden pole fixed upright and covered with bristly coconut-matting doormats. Daisy and Pip stood side by side with the post between them, wriggling and

grunting as they rubbed their broad
rumps against the bristles.

Sam gave a cheer. "They love it!"

"They love everything here," said
Amelia. "It's perfect." The pigpen had
plenty of room for Daisy and Pip to
wander, and lots of grass for them to
root about in.

Mrs Parish gave a satisfied nod. "They're settling in nicely. I'm so glad we were able to adopt them. It was a great idea, Amelia."

Caleb grinned. "I can't believe we've got two pigs now, as well as the llamas. Not long ago we didn't have any pets, and now we've got four big ones!"

"You've almost got enough for a petting farm!" said Amelia, laughing.

Mr and Mrs Parish didn't say anything, but Amelia thought she saw them exchange a look.

Hmm, she thought. *Maybe that's not a bad idea!*

"Well," said Annie, "we'd better say goodbye to our giant micro pigs." She and Kate rubbed Daisy and Pip's ears and fed them a few bits of piggy flapjack. "Bye, bye, piggies. We'll visit whenever we can."

"You're welcome any time," said Mrs Parish, smiling.

"Thank you," said Kate. "We'll miss

them, but we know they'll be much happier here. And now Tammy and Tim have all the room they need."

Annie checked the time on her phone. "We'd better hurry. We've got to go and replant the flowerbed on the village green that the pigs spoilt!"

Mr and Mrs Hope arrived just as
the ladies left. The vets strode around
the pigpen, smiling broadly. "What a
fantastic pig house!" said Mrs Hope.
"It's just perfect. Daisy and Pip are very
lucky."

"Yes," said Mr Hope. "You've done
Animal Ark proud."

"Thank you," said Amelia. She
thought her heart would burst with
happiness. Sam grinned and she high-
fived him. "Actually, Mr and Mrs Hope,
now that Daisy and Pip have more
space, there's something else I wanted to
ask you about …"

"Surprise!" shouted Amelia, when Lena and Sofia opened their front door a short while later.

"What do you think?" said Sam. He was holding a hamster cage and Amelia carried a box of freshly baked hamster treats.

The twins stared at them, confused.

"I did some research," explained Amelia. "It turns out hamsters are happier living alone. I checked with Mr and Mrs Hope and they agreed – and they gave us this spare cage."

"So now Nibbles can have his own home," added Sam.

"And Nacho can't steal his food," said Amelia.

"That's brilliant!" said Lena.

"Let's put him in his new home right away," said Sofia.

They trooped upstairs, and it was Amelia's turn to be surprised. The bunk beds had gone, and instead there were two new beds on opposite sides of the room. One was still a mess, the other perfectly made, but there was a clear space in the middle of the room.

"Mum and Dad got them for us," said Lena. "It's really nice to have our own beds."

"Lena's stopped mixing all her stuff up with mine," said Sofia.

Lena reached down to pick up a teddy on the neat side. She put it on the messy bed and said, "Well, almost." The twins looked at each other and laughed.

Amelia smiled at Sam. The twins had stopped squabbling now they had their own space, and hopefully the hamsters would be happier too. *Like Daisy and Pip!*

Sam put the new cage next to the old one, where Nibbles and Nacho were curled up asleep. Lena and Sofia got it ready, putting sawdust on the floor and bedding in the nesting box.

Then Sofia picked up the tub of

hamster treats. She rattled it, and
Nibbles and Nacho woke up. They
yawned and sat by the bars of their
cage, whiskers twitching.

Lena grinned. "They love these treats!"
She lifted Nibbles out and put him inside
the new cage. Nibbles stood very still
for a moment, as if deciding whether he
liked it. Then he began to explore. He
sniffed each corner carefully.

"Here, Nibbles. Your first treat in your
new home." Sofia gave Nibbles one of
the hamster treats. He clutched it in his
front paws and chewed it happily.

"Can we give Nacho
one too?" asked Sam.

"Only a little bit," said Sofia, breaking a piece off. "Mr Hope says he's too heavy because he was eating all of Nibbles's food. He's on a diet now."

The hamsters gobbled up their treats. Afterwards, Nibbles explored his new cage, while Nacho sat and groomed himself. He licked every crumb off his little pink paws before briskly washing

his face and ears.

"Right," said Sam. "I've got to walk Mac. Who's coming?"

"Me!" said Lena, jumping up. "Let's take him to the park."

"The park's rubbish!" said Sofia. "I vote for the woods."

"Why don't we go to the park first, then the woods?" said Amelia.

Both sisters nodded.

As the twins went downstairs to put on their shoes, Amelia and Sam followed.

"They still can't agree on anything," whispered Sam.

"I think that's what sisters are like sometimes," Amelia replied with a grin. As she closed the bedroom door, she glanced back at Nibbles and Nacho, happy in their separate cages.

*At least we can all agree on one thing –
helping animals is the best feeling ever!*

The End

Turn the page for a sneak peek at
Amelia and Sam's next adventure!

ANIMAL ARK

Guinea Pig Superstar

Lucy Daniels

On the screen, an adorable smoky-grey kitten sprang into action, standing on its back paws in front of a mirror, shadow boxing with its own image. It bopped and pawed at the glass, its fluffy fur sticking up on end. Then the kitten hunkered down, wiggled its tiny backside and pounced. It hit the mirror, bounced off and scrambled away, its feet skittering in every direction.

Mac let out an excited bark. Sam and Amelia giggled.

"That's so adorable!" Amelia said. Then she turned to Sam. "Hey! Maybe *we* should make some funny pet videos for the Animal Ark website."

"That's not a bad idea!" Mr Hope said, carrying an armful of supplies from the store cupboard. "We haven't updated the site for a while. We want to make it fun and friendly to attract new customers to the surgery. A few animal videos might be just what's needed." He put down his bundle. "I'll lend you an old phone to take some clips."

Amelia squeezed her hands together with excitement. Sam's eyes shone. "There are so many cool animals in Welford, we're bound to make some epic videos!" he said.

Read Guinea Pig Superstar to find out what happens next ...

Animal Advice

Do you love animals as much as Amelia and Sam? Here are some tips on how to look after them from veterinary surgeon Sarah McGurk.

Caring for your pet

1 Animals need clean water at all times.

2 They need to be fed too – ask your vet what kind of food is best, and how much the animal needs.

3 Some animals, such as dogs, need exercise every day.

4 Animals also need lots of love. You should always be very gentle with your pets and be careful not to do anything that might hurt them.

When to go to the vet

Sometimes animals get ill. Like you, they will mostly get better on their own. But if your pet has hurt itself or seems very unwell, then a trip to the vet might be needed. Some pets also need to be vaccinated, to prevent them from getting dangerous diseases. Your vet can tell you what your pet needs.

Helping wildlife

1 Always ask an adult before you go near any animals you don't know.

2 If you find an animal or bird which is injured or can't move, it is best not to touch it.

3 If you are worried, you can phone an animal charity such as the RSPCA (SSPCA in Scotland) for help.